Stars Along My Back

Stars Along My Back

Poems

Christina White

Wild Rising Press

EVERGREEN, COLORADO

Cover Design: Mary M. Meade & Judyth Hill with use of photo by jessicahyde/via IStock
Book Design: Mary M. Meade
Editor: Judyth Hill

wildrisingpress.com
ISBN 978-1-957468-14-3—First Edition

To my Creator and all my parents.

The ones that saved me, the ones that kept me alive,

and the ones that broke me into a thousand pieces.

I am grateful for your deep lessons.

Contents

Stars

Along

My

Back

A Lover's Blanket

In the night
darkness blankets me as a splendid furry mantle,
protecting too-fragile skin from the light.

Weeping sap and vulnerability.

Ancient wounds created long ago.
Tender, moist, raw and wet.

Too soft and wounded to touch the light

    yet.

It's a miracle to me
how the Love of light falls into places, filling creases in pillows and
Hearts.

Giant mountaintops
blanketed with snow glisten.

Fur shines alongside rivers
petite black shiny noses, shimmer.

Skirting across glass, brightness
and grassy bamboo shades.

Sounds shift butterfly wings … liquid elixirs glide in the light.

Carving stone.
Bleaching bones.

The stillest air inviting birdsong.

Why not?
Why not play the instrument among the leaves and branches?

Flowers bloom as imprints left … kissing moonlight on necks of

delicate down feathers.

Lips brush away the silence in ears.

Whispering secrets

only true lovers know.

Last Night

A young monk enjoyed playing with his hair.

Shy fingers twirled
around sacred temples
waking up silken thread.

He tickled his forehead
                    loving it again.

Negotiations went on forever.

Wondering about dispersing particles in the dark, grids and positions of
    letters,
languages of sand.

The threads you weave with your hand
in the loom upon my invisible bed.

Did I choose this?
Yes—

I did.

Before it all started.

The path was under me, falling to the place without floors.
Lost in the night,
feet going nowhere.

Exploding.

Eventually, his skin left me shattered.

The smallest particle of myself
laid down in the sky.

Lips parted full.

The green blanket covered my thighs and nipples
shoulders & neck.

Steam rose from my hands.

Vessels of womb steam rising.

Blood.

Orange, pink, red and blue
rose
meeting
the sky.

Infinite eyes.
Peacock-colored purple jewel eyes.

Last Night II

I licked bone marrow from a spoon.

Hot silk melted in my mouth.
Rolling down the sides
of my tongue.

Buttered bread
sour & toasted perfectly soft with crisp edges.
Tickled with the tips of parsley.

Tender treetops crunched between my teeth

endlessly.

In the Desert

Something is happening.

Stone stillness.
Grey granite far away, smells of overbaked sourdough rye

releasing arid vestiges of its last steam ether.

Flammable creosote gathers fire from the sun moon.

Night mice hide in tunnels alongside sandy granite creeks,
remembering rain,

crying tears of
what was once another liquid flowing through veins.

Dark blue thunderstorms

strike cracks of hope for black crawly things that only come out at night

in the desert.

Father

No, I won't tell the trolls or ghouls my secrets.

While I make marmalade jelly
even if they knew,
it would be rotten before it fell

                        carelessly into the wrong soil.

Broken eggs.

Attempting to fool itself …
believing
it was safe
from the fires
        under the heavy
                seasoned, ancient frying pan

resting.
Ready,
upon the salted stove.

Eventually—
jeweled sticky fingers lick hell like it was a cinnamon bun.

Fools.

You thought I was sorting seeds
and I was sorting stars.

Digestive juice dripping from my mouth

throat squeezes
with intention.

Drop.

Thinking—
I never saw a thing.

When your blade was dull
I felt the crunch.

When the pasta was lost I felt the
milky mush.

When the water was wrong
I felt the cloud.

Joints ache & teeth stick,

Eyes blur.

Life is short and
it whispers to me

make marmalade jelly
& give it all

away.

The Stone Path

Stone feet yearn …

Toes reach, touching invisibility.

I feel your warmth,
                tender in the Morning Sun
shooting up the back of my legs.

The insides of things move imperceptibly.

Black and Light exist in shadow
nothing
moves through me

Except
toes lean into
your hard surface
smooth or rough
discovering its limits
again.

My femur connects
pushing through

skin.

Tendon and muscle,

Yes!

You are still there—
pushing.

Hips and belly.
You are still there,

vibrating inside Womb and Heart echoing in chambers
as the most still blue lake.

You are still there…

Echoing.

Zinc, manganese, boron & calcium
you are still there with my ancestors.
Spines compress fluid and breath

between
two spheres.

Bone and flesh.

You are still there as
fish whirl
catching water nymphs
above,
filling bellies.

Eggs drop protection for you.

Stay still.

   Possible crack,

blessings for creation seek refuge.

You are there—
solitude and respite from the chaotic predators hiding in darkness.

Roads, cobbles and stone travel.
Lie still and strong
giant mountain.

Among many you are sparkling.
You are still there!

Under toe or saddle,
my femur …

Essence coats the nose with the dust of eons walking.
Raw organic minerals crumble … along your path,
knees rise to meet the mountain—

under my femur.

Once

I tried to write a Poem—

Choruses heard in songs refusing to leave my head.

"Are we in Love?" it said.

Nothing dripped from eternity …

Silent bombs.

I want to read other people's poems
but I'll fall in love.

Then …

There is nothing I can do.

Nothing
never
comes.

This Morning

A hummingbird flew—

Behind the head of my husband
drinking nectar and licking it
from the bright

pink
salvias.

Wings beat like thunder.

He sat still in his chair.

Drinking *betabel* juice and eating eggs

I made him

                              —for breakfast

Created

I was formed by irrigation
from the Verde River.

Poured into Indian ditches
long ago.

Low dangerous—
cactus
ocotillo
orange marigolds, corn, beans
        and
white bread.

Pima cotton fields growing clouds of storms.

My mother prayed to Hannah,
                my father was lost in space, distracted by the stars.

My great-grandmother formed my tongue on
violet concord jelly jars, topped with copper pennies.

Coyotes were my friends as a four-legged hoofed spider
carried me

Alone.

Along the path
illuminated by the elegant Moon
Round and Full.

Listening.

Formed by the creosote that catches fire easily.
Piñon pine-filled lungs,
strength & passion.

Reaching.

Formed by abandonment stones let loose.

     Dragging,

kicking
and
screaming

and drowning

in blankets I made by threads of grass that I lay on.

On the shore of the Verde River
as my horse grazed.

Then I was born on a buffalo rug on the Mogollon Rim.

I am the firm corn bursting in the mouth
of the tiny garden outside
Grandmother's window.

Milk exploding between teeth.

Sweet apples hiding in the back of her dark closet
behind her cooled room.

The damp
square
shiny

metal
swamp
cooler
connected
to the locksmith shop.

My grandfather Chet
left,
a lot …

    Forming me.

Apples
plums
puppies
kittens
on a farm did too.

A Man
loving deeply.

Giving space for stars.

Remembering forming
flowers
before he forgot …

I remembered.

Ode to the Dawn

Death brushed against the bamboo threads.

Soft and silky,
weaving the way
around,

hours & bones.

Waiting for Dawn.

… Creeping inwards and through
creamy draperies hung last night.

Trying to keep it at bay,
short, green sprouts
crept in anyway.

Beginning to glow a beautiful orange pink warmth … outside.

Eyes like silk.

Opening before the Dawn.

You were there.

Teasing me.

Emptiness

Skies and honking cars
barking dogs and bars.

Clouds that rain thunderously.

The top of my head

and Mount Everest.

Cold.

Unreachable
as I lie in bed.

The Garden Dripping with Fruit

In darkness
the moths came, tiny ones that had been waiting …

Barely visible little bodies before they are born

Night Butterflies.

Bright candles dripping.
Teeth & licking.

Dark grass.

Padding cloud paws.

Stretching necks.

Sweat.

Claws at the doorstep,
Water dripping down my back.

Splitting wood and thighs.

Making Night Butterflies.

Across the Street

Bitterness might live.
Unhealthy & bloated
screaming.

What?!

Now & then I see someone try to help.

Dropping her off a cliff
again.

Surprised exhaustion, had a party last month
not inviting any neighbors
into the rented house. Old music played,
young, innocent women danced

on rooftops, entertaining small men …

Everyone left early.
No one went in.
The decorations stayed up

… wilting.

The next morning trying to rise from her bed, petals fell.

Beautiful arrangements
made by Artists for her—

Small yellow butterflies surfed
in the air with nowhere to land—

daring her …

to land.

Good Morning Sunshine!

Your mother called last night.

Saying
"I miss you."

She can't remember
bad times.
"Life

is

    all

        new."

Inviting me to swim
upon the shore.

Pause and become inward
once more …

Saying—*"I love You."*

A giant blue octopus was with her
swirling all around
reaching out—

"You won't drown, she's not here
anymore, she's walking around town …

a giant seagull beak
always open
screaming to be filled with

black cave bellies full of stones that weigh all the way down."

"She's not here anymore.
She flew away
somewhere far."

Imagining …
seashells on the shoreline, sand under calloused feet.

Forever
searching for treasures.

Once

I knew a man
trying to understand why something broke.

Massive floods came from the corner of the eye.

Escaping to the hills I cried in silence.

A Man alone.

No one can own something stolen.

Its fire sits between worlds,
crying out to families trying to forge steel.

He's out …
oops (she's) now out …

of recycled material.

What grows well in my garden

Little peppers.

Hot.
Although simple, do not.

Marigolds, cosmos, corn, onions & apples take root.

Grandmothers align gold seeds.

Gritty soil full of small stones,
squash & beans.

Orange blossom, duck & venison.

Fine Lace, pink & blue
velvet cotton ribbon.

Cypress & Ficus nearly grow in the dark.

Fine china or clay eagerly line up upon shelves, waiting for the
Harvesting of dawn … plums
fields of marigolds & Colorado Sun.

Resting under the shade of Jonathan's—
Apple trees.

Chickens & dogs.
Pillows.
Blankets.

More baskets than I can count—

Full Hearts.

A drunk life

and soul-filled barrels of titanium-puddled sunflower seeds nestled
    between tightly woven bowls

of pine needle trees.

Grandmother's Star fingers

Sorting seeds.

The Mountaintop

Large velvet buttercream pillows thrown carelessly on the bed.

Silk pillow behind my head.

Linen draperies wrap me like clouds, I'm on the tops
of mountains.

Below me are
verdant towering cypress scattered about

quiet sound.

Keeping the House Clean

It's impossible to keep a House clean.

Rooms closed off.
Sitting.

Fresh rotten strawberries that sat in the refrigerator
unused.
Mold.

Dark, cold and lifeless, sheets crisp, unwrinkled, sterile and
stale as dust.

No mop or broom or white cloth, no air or spider.
Laugh, smile
or
beautiful stains.

Sitting still as death, a museum cluttered and overflowing.
Dense petrified atoms.

Carcasses, stuffed things with no soul, covered in hair and fur.
Glass eyeballs staring past me.
Going nowhere.

Draperies, silk reins of doubt.
Caging everything in.

Keeping life out.

Stand up to Death

Quickly! —Kill it …

—wait—

and then …

when it's not looking—

Again

Sharp knife,

needle arrow

Searing heat and stone coldness.

DONE.

Don't push it away—

Invite it in!

Then … Kill it …

A smile,
grinning
white teeth
open hands
worm castings & soil.

Fresh seeds.

Ancestors open mouths
flowers fall
giving birth.

Again.

The Kiss

You kissed me.
Long ago, it seems.

Minds wander off, splitting seams.
Full orbs and pink necks
begin to stretch into vulnerable hands.

Rip.

Gentle and ravenous was every concise move,
gravitational worlds begin to swirl,

ripe words—
ring true in ears stuffed with fields of white Pima cotton.

Eyes walked, balancing along two worlds with no memory of what
    precisely happened.

Heavily, peacefully and gently could I have died,

lying on the warm green grass with you by the cold river at night.

Wet

Grass is silky with dew longing in the dawn.
It remembers the waiting and misunderstandings.

Black with charred ash of pasts. Stale seeds left
long in a dark closet.

Indiscretions grow and reach to the sky like potato seeds in a closet.

Uninhibited.

Unlatching windows late at night.

White paint cracking on the front pine doorframe, the one with the four
     windowpanes and the golden latch.

Sheer cotton curtains brushed the top of my wrist as I turned the locked
     knob trying to let you in.

Security doesn't exist.

Flesh dances in the mud trying to be as simple as earth in the sandy
     desert.

Silhouettes shiver
silver linings—for clouds across dark blue pools

and sheer window coverings,

I got this.

Gathered together with the linen tied in a bow, woven hemp

long ago, raw and beautifully natural against the limestone & the smell
of your   life   blood

and cats howling in alleys lined with pomegranate trees and wild orange
    mallow.

Warning me with sounds—
of the water droplets in your breath rubbing into my skin forcing my
    cells to sweat for you

again …

Waiting for something
that doesn't feel the urgency,

Yet.

Your Love a second ago
has rolled off as

morning dew.

The Song

Where do the birds go when it storms?

Maybe down in the grass snuggling among golden mountainous wheat
    fields where it begins to sprout up into tufts.

Quivering feathers … fluff balls of bodies within golden straw wheat
    dust.

Puffing feathers
as a mother's breasts do
when they fill with milk.

Where do the birds go when they are sick?

Maybe they hide under the leaves
covering little heads and tucked beaks.

Bowing in vulnerability as a Father
when he sees a human child being born.

                    Waiting for eternity.

Fragile moments holding
the thinnest already-cracked glass.

Endlessly listening … fragile attempts to protect it from the shattering
    winds of time
and change.

In awe of the Earth.

Where do birds go when they sing?

I know.

They sit in trees lifting their heads
stretching necks, opening mouth beaks
as though to receive a breath from God,

and turn it

into song.

Water

He will show you the crown waiting for your head.
Then attempt to replace the one already
upon it.

He will show you emptiness … the feeling of dread.

He will show you nothing, darkness emptied as the sea.

He is not allowed to have
sovereignty.

Over hands
feet
heart
meat
ear
eye
mouth
thigh.

This place, this body reigns
strong.

Light in hand.
Vessel secure and unbreakable
wet and slipping.

Everywhere.

They will tell you to create space by taking it away.

No boundaries
leaves you weightless and without gravity.

He will tell you nothing
leaving you stillborn

Alone.

He will tell you empty words

void of stone.

What happens

when God writes you a poem?

Falling to knees, all plastic melts
& decays.

That Beautiful vanity …
Grandmother gave,
    —Falls
The dovetails give way.

Away color runs, lines blur.

Metabolic shifts occur.
Stubborn mountains, the black granite hourglass.

Nothing is new.

Only—
Rose-colored veils used to protect us from the scorching sun.

The Leaf Drifts

In spring,
sap ascends.

Strawberries pick lips.
Red stains on hips, the strawberry leaf drifts—

cottonwoods spawn.
Blankets of warm spring mantles
drift upon green grass …

Bowls of bunnies snuggle beneath straw bales.
Tunnels of Love fur, tender and new.
Baby down & pink skin.

Leaf's drift—

In summer,
thick, wide rivers flow
heavy and steadily.

Finches celebrate second nests.

Midnights deliver uninterrupted silence, generously seasoned with
cricket violins.

Inevitably
the random leaf drifts.

In the fall
cold air grabs the last of the leaves.
Brown paper wisps.

Rain gutters jam, filled with ice … alongside the irrigation trench.

In winter, sap swells trunks with sweetness, until the fall
leaves.

42

…

Christina drifts.

Hours

Pussy Rocks and Cock Flowers

Sky, Earth or Hours

Time doesn't exist.
Except for the moon upon my hearth.

I want.

Feeling a lover's kiss upon my neck devours me whole from the insides
    out.

Drop muscle and flesh.

Insides melt.

Bite and chew my feet apart.

Opening.
Stars along my back.

Streaking through the sky in ecstasy
with nowhere to go

Free

Acknowledgements

First, I would like to thank Judyth Hill, my editor with incredible vision, who saw me in the Dark, Mary Meade, for her art direction and creative genius—and collectively, Judyth and Mary, as Wild Rising Press, for producing and publishing this book.

Leslie, who gave me a key that lifted the veil.

Jonathan, my incredible husband of nearly 40 years, who supported me as I walked through a new door & David, who showed us the way to it.

Michaela, who ignited my senses & Sofia (everywhere you are), who held my hand and showed me I was not alone.

Lastly, but not the least …
the Blooming Desert at Night and my fur-covered friends.

Author's Biography

Christina Renee White is the granddaughter of a highly decorated Air Force war hero and the daughter of a Space Hall of Fame member. Her mother is an artist and math teacher. Her lineage has been traced back to the last French Monarchy and, even further, to Copernicus. Her journey reflects the indomitable spirit of the survival of Beauty, Sensuality, Generosity, and Strength.

She grew up in the Upper Sonoran Desert riding her horse "Spider" at night, exploring the wild, untamed Southwest without supervision. Her adolescence was a time of emotional turmoil, marked by periods of deep understanding...facilitated by her Grandmothers, who nurtured an inner sanctum of creativity and Beauty that became her saving grace.

Her life has, at times, been a song of recklessness, abandonment, and betrayal seasoned with understanding and rebirth. It is the song of every strong Woman who looks deeply within herself to unravel authentic expression as the source and strength for living a life of Truth frosted with a deep sensuality.

This petite book of poetry sings the call of the beginning chapter in a journey of the arising of the spirit of feminine flight.

Christina White lives and writes in the ancient city of San Miguel de Allende and the mountains of Colorado. This is her first book.

Adobe Garamond was chosen for the text of these poems…and Arno Pro Light for the poems' titles. Garamond, delicate, refined, not just a single typeface but a group of fonts dating back to the 16th century, was designed to echo the grace of the skillful hand wielding pen and ink. This font supports the exquisite tension between the refined musicality and luscious—and often fierce—sensuality of the poems. The title font, Arno, named for the Italian river flowing, sometimes a torrent, from the Apennines through Florence, into the sea…speaks to the urgency and passion of the Voice behind this work.